D1530040

ME AND YOU AND THE UNIVERSE

WRITTEN AND ILLUSTRATED BY
BERNARDO MARÇOLLA

free spirit
PUBLISHING®

Library of Congress Cataloging-in-Publication Data
Names: Marçolla, Bernardo Andrade, 1973- author, illustrator.
Title: Me and you and the universe / written and illustrated by Bernardo Marçolla.
Description: Minneapolis, MN : Free Spirit Publishing Inc., [2020] |
Identifiers: LCCN 2019038761 (print) | LCCN 2019038762 (ebook) | ISBN 9781631985225 (hardcover) | ISBN 9781631985232 (pdf) |
        ISBN 9781631985249 (epub)
Subjects: LCSH: Life (Biology)—Juvenile literature.
Classification: LCC QH309.2 .M37 2020 (print) | LCC QH309.2 (ebook) | DDC 570--dc23
LC record available at https://lccn.loc.gov/2019038761
LC ebook record available at https://lccn.loc.gov/2019038762

Free Spirit Publishing does not have control over or assume responsibility for author or third-party websites and their content.

Reading Level Grade 3
Fountas & Pinnell Guided Reading Level P

Edited by Alison Behnke
Cover and interior design by Shannon Pourciau

10 9 8 7 6 5 4 3 2 1
Printed in China
R18861119

Free Spirit Publishing Inc.
6325 Sandburg Road, Suite 100
Minneapolis, MN 55427-3674
(612) 338-2068
help4kids@freespirit.com
freespirit.com

FSC
www.fsc.org
MIX
Paper from
responsible sources
FSC® C144853

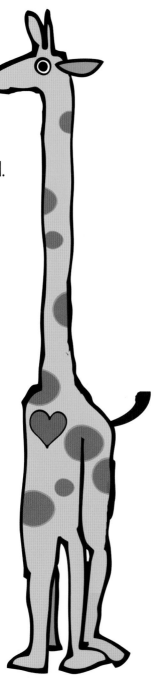

DEDICATION

To Nature and all her creatures, the great and the small.

ACKNOWLEDGMENTS

I would like to express my gratitude to everyone who helped make this book a reality, especially to my sister Nanda, my wife Adriane, and the whole Free Spirit Publishing team. Beyond that, my deepest gratitude to the dreams that inhabit us, because without them nothing would be possible.

Once upon a time there was a
beautiful planet named Earth...

... and Earth had something very special
that had not yet been discovered anywhere else.

What existed on this planet that was so special?

LIFE!

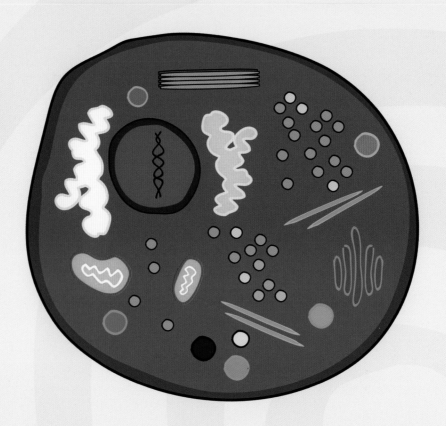

The smallest form of life we know is the cell. A cell is so small that when it is by itself, we cannot even see it. But cells can multiply.

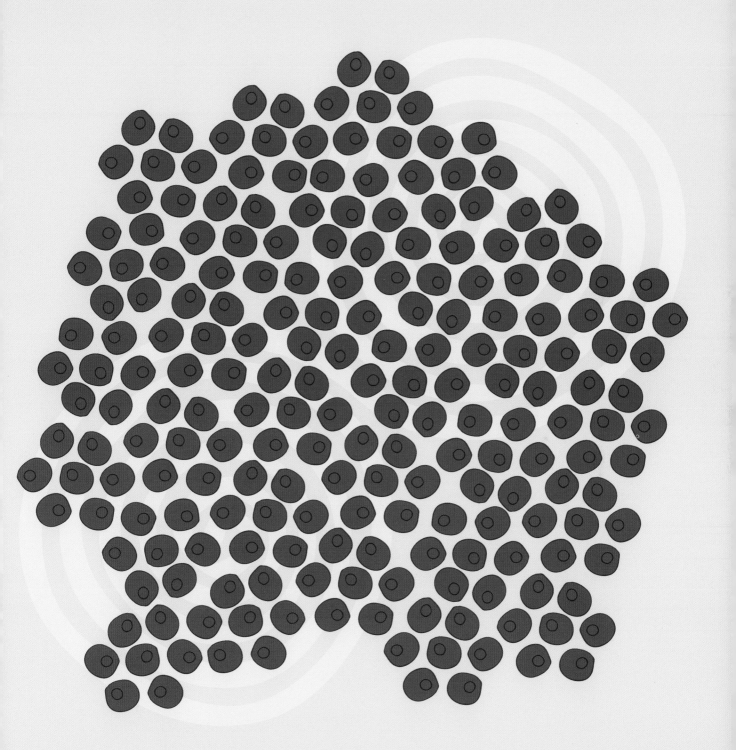

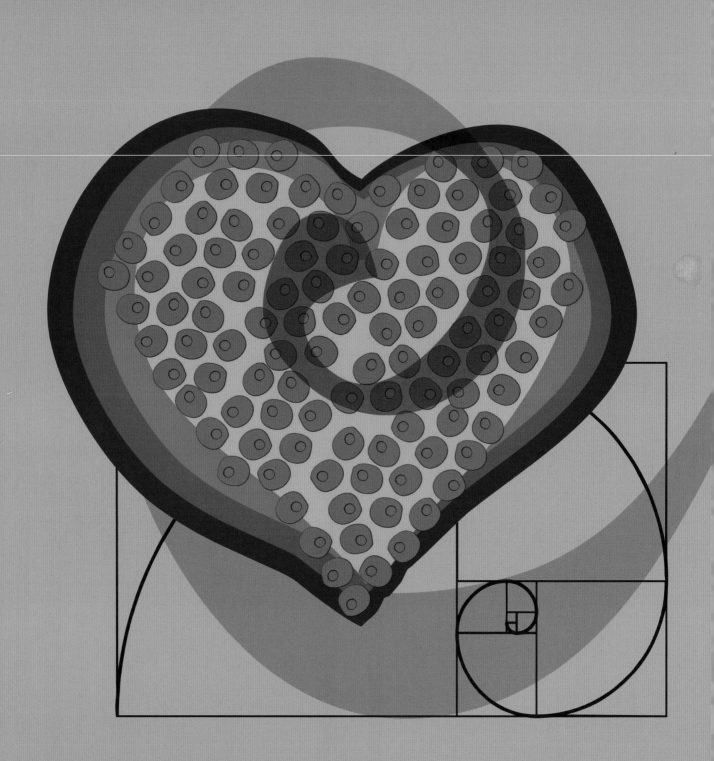

Cells are like tiny building blocks.
They come together to form all
the parts of all living things.

Although we sometimes seem different from other people and other creatures, all of us, deep down inside, are very similar.

Of all the special creatures that live on Earth,
humans think a lot about the ways we are different.

And we ARE all different in some ways.

There are people with a few curves and people with a lot of curves.
People who are young and people who are old.

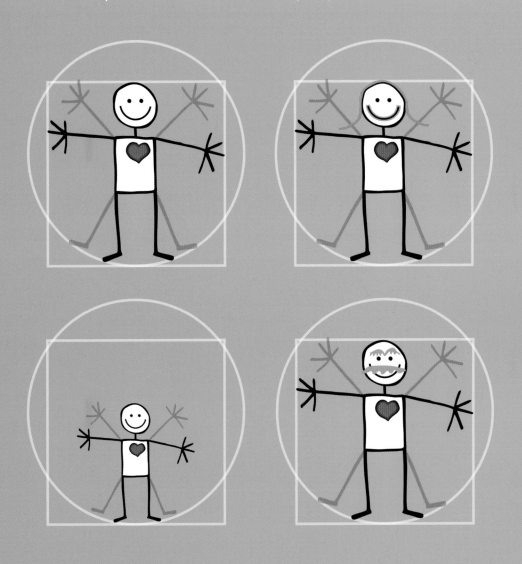

There are tall and short people.
Those who eat salad and those who LOVE chocolate.

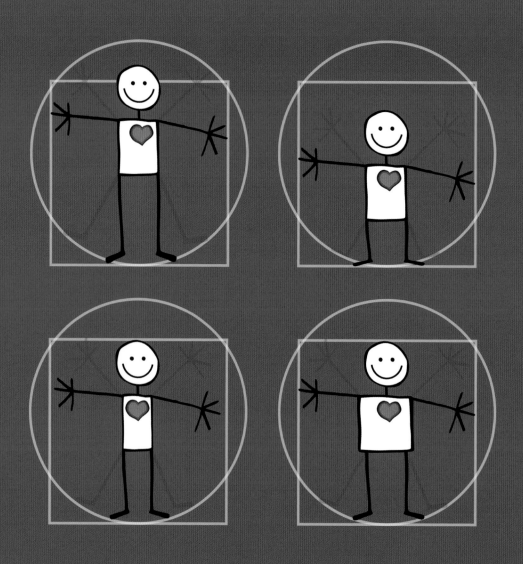

People are like works of art.
We come in many colors and shapes, and we are each unique.

There are people who are born as kings and those
who learn by themselves to have magic and power.

There are fashionable people and those who feel so different
that they wonder if they have come from another planet.

But none of these differences is so important.

What is REALLY important is to begin to notice how the various parts of ourselves can pull us in different directions.

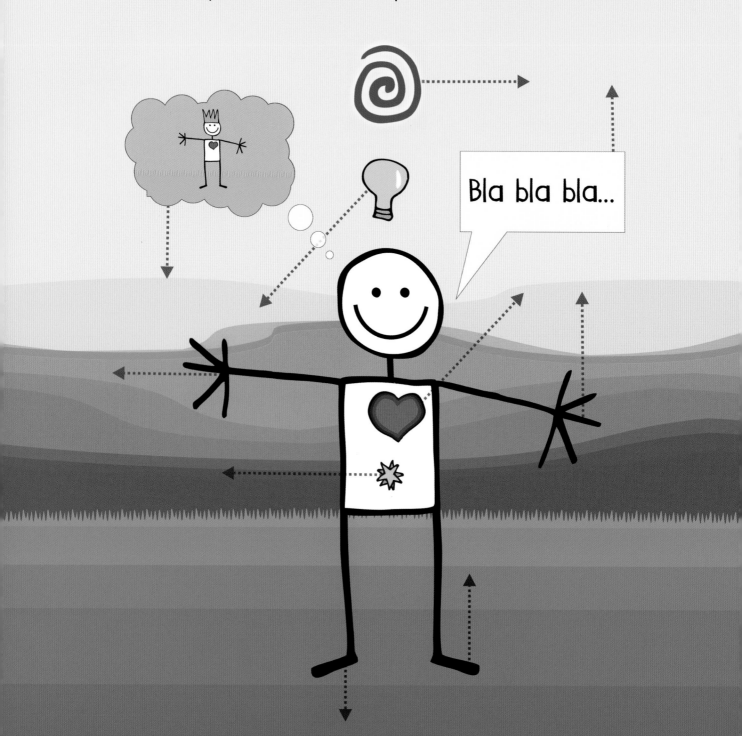

Are your body, your heart, your ideas, your dreams, your desires, your speech, your actions, and your spirit all in tune?

It turns out that when we are out of tune within ourselves, it is really hard (really, really, REALLY hard!) to truly connect with other people.

Until we understand ourselves, it's almost impossible
to clearly see and understand others.

But if we look inside and get to know each bit
of ourselves, things will slowly become clearer.

This is the greatest (and the best) labor of our lives.

It is how we learn to know and fully relate to other people, with both our light and our shadow.

Then we can really know and relate to ALL beings.

We realize WE ARE ALL ONE.
And now we can look at our planet in a completely new way.

THE EARTH IS A LIVING BEING.

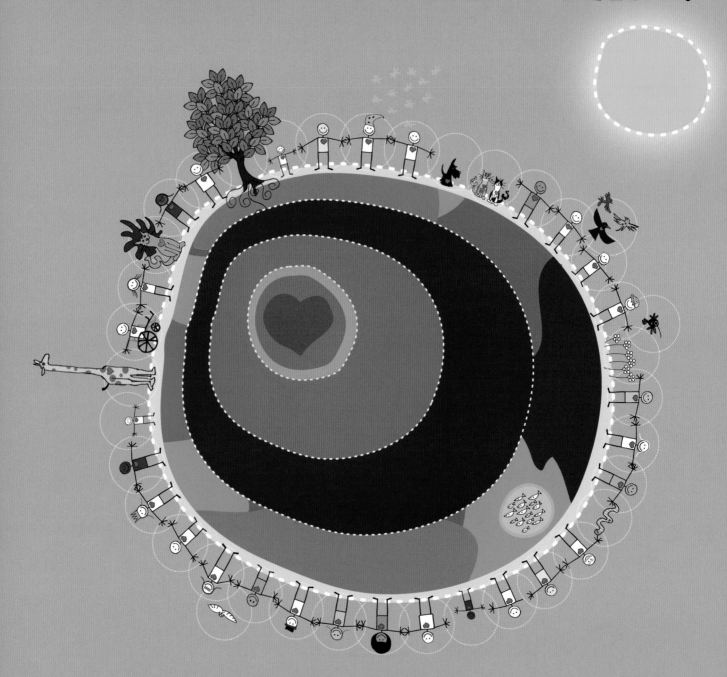

(And it has its own heart!)

Then we can go even further . . .

. . . and discover that we are all part
of something much bigger, which
moves in rhythms of great harmony.

We can see that we are each a tiny
part of a universe that is INFINITE.

(It does not even fit in this book!)

We find that everything is connected . . .

and maybe we will start asking new questions

And that will be the beginning of so many new and beautiful stories.

A NOTE FROM BERNARDO

As you were reading this book, you thought about the way you interact with nature and the larger world. About how you interact with others—and with yourself. About how you are a part of the universe. When you consider these ideas, you open yourself up to a whole new way of thinking and living.

Often, we build walls. Sometimes we even do this as a way of trying to protect nature, or ourselves, or those we love. Although our intentions are good, our actions often do not lead to the desired effects—in nature or in ourselves.

As human beings, we too rarely think of our own nature, and we can forget that the way we relate to the outside world is a reflection of how we relate to ourselves. We forget that we are *part* of nature, and we become fragmented—disconnected from our own inner ecology. We are divided within ourselves, and the relationships we build with other people and with other beings are fragile as a result.

It can even feel as though we're living with blindfolds at times, struggling to see all the beauty that surrounds us. Too often, we don't notice the colors of the sunset; we ignore the amazing processes that transform a seed into a tree or a flower; we forget that before being born we are quite similar to many other creatures. And if we are blind to what is visible around us, imagine how difficult it is to see the invisible and hidden things inside ourselves.

Of course, maybe we were not taught to see clearly. This is not our fault. Yet we can take responsibility for healing ourselves and making a change. We have to look inside and outside ourselves to see everything within us and around us. In doing so, our actions will naturally change. Our own consciousness has a voice, and it speaks to us.

It is important for all of us—at any age—to learn to listen to this voice, to look up to the sky, and, as we see the stars, to *know* that we are part of them. This is a wisdom that is completely different from the knowledge that comes from studying and degrees. It is not the most elaborate reasoning that will change the way we see the world or ourselves. Instead, the answer is wonderfully simple: We have to open our eyes and open our hearts. The world will remain the same, but our experience will be completely changed. *We* will be changed.

ABOUT THE AUTHOR
AND ILLUSTRATOR

BERNARDO MARÇOLLA is an author and illustrator who holds a doctorate and postdoctorate in literature, as well as a master's degree in psychology, and who has more than ten years of experience as a professor of psychology. Since 2012, he has been an analyst in the Human Resources area of the Brazilian Institute of Geography and Statistics, and in 2017, he published the book *Psychology and Ecology: Nature, Subjectivity and Its Intersections* (in Portuguese). Inspired to adapt the ideas in that book for children, Bernardo created *Me and You and the Universe*. He loves chocolate and still has not given up on learning to draw a little better. He lives in Belo Horizonte, Brazil, with his wife and two cats.